To my **dearest**

A little something
to show you just how much

I love you.

Illustrations created by Caroline Keys, inspired by May Gibbs' original works.

Published by Scholastic Australia in 2024.

Scholastic Australia Pty Limited
PO Box 579 Gosford NSW 2250
ABN 11 000 614 577
www.scholastic.com.au

Part of the Scholastic Group
Sydney • Auckland • New York • Toronto • London • Mexico City • New Delhi
Hong Kong • Buenos Aires • Puerto Rico

Designer: Stephanie Olive | Editor: Hannah Janssen

ISBN 978-1-76026-669-1

Printed in China.

Scholastic Australia's policy, in association with its printers, is to use papers that are renewable and made effi ciently from wood grown in responsibly managed forests, so as to minimise its environmental footprint.

All the Love in the Bush

SCHOLASTIC
SYDNEY AUCKLAND NEW YORK TORONTO LONDON MEXICO CITY
NEW DELHI HONG KONG BUENOS AIRES PUERTO RICO

One day, Snugglepot and Cuddlepie were walking through the bush.

They were the closest two Gumnuts could be.
But Snugglepot could not help but wonder . . .

'**Cuddlepie** . . . how much do you **love** me?'

Cuddlepie thought hard. How could he even begin to explain?

'I love you . . .

. . . and ALL the petals
on their blossoms!’

'Wow!' exclaimed Snugglepot. That was a lot.
'Well,' he began,

'I love you . . .

more than ALL the scales
on Mr Lizard's back!'

Cuddlepie giggled. This was his favourite game to play.

'My love for you . . .

is **softer** than a baby possum's fur.'

‘And I **love you**

higher than Mrs Kangaroo can jump.’

'I love you more than *all* the **gumnuts** on *all* of the branches.'

‘I love you **sweeter** than all the **honey** in the bush.’

‘I love you **more** than all the

butterflies in the sky.'

‘I love you more than the most **beautiful** ballet.’

'I love you **further** than the frogs can leap on their **lily pads.**'

‘I
love
you
deeper
than
the
river.’

‘I love you more than all the
fireflies in the
billabong.’

'I love you **taller** than the highest **treetop.**'

'I love you **brighter** than the sun!'

'My love for you is

stronger . . .

than the

mightiest gumtree.'

'My love for you burns ***warmer*** than a blazing **campfire.'**

'I love you **fluffier** than all of
Mrs Kookaburra's feathers!'

The Gumnuts rolled around laughing.
'How do you love someone *fluffily?*'
Cuddlepie asked.

Snugglepot wondered. 'I think I love you

more than words can explain.'

Cuddlepie agreed. 'I love you more than

all the love in the Bush.'